Four small chairs
just right for bears.
Where is the bear
for each small chair?

Calico Bear
sits on a chair.
He likes it there
on his one chair.

Now Fuzzy Bear
wants a chair.
She climbs up there
on the second chair.

Another chair
is over there.
Yellow Bear
takes that chair.

Here's Floppy Bear.
She takes a chair.
She's happy there
on that last chair.

Four happy bears
on four small chairs.

Not a bear
has to share.

Oops!

Big Brown Bear
looks for a chair.
There is none there
for that big bear.

What a stare
from Big Brown Bear.
That big bear
wants a chair!

Can Big Brown Bear
make a pair
with Floppy Bear
on her one chair?

No, Floppy Bear
and that big bear
cannot share
one small chair.

That big bear
needs one whole chair.
There's none to spare
for Big Brown Bear.

Look!

Calico Bear
shifts his chair
over there
near Big Brown Bear.

Big Brown Bear
helps Calico Bear
make one double chair
for three to share.

Oh no!

Two of the bears
fall off that chair!
That double chair
can't hold three bears.

Fuzzy Bear
looks over there.
She scoots her chair
beside the pair.

Now Yellow Bear
scoots his chair.
Will one long chair
hold all those bears?

First Big Brown Bear,
then Yellow Bear,
climb up there
on that long chair.

The other bears
look over there.
Is there room to spare
for three more bears?

Yes!

There's room up there
for all *five* bears!
Now it's fair!
The bears all share!

For all my granddaughters,
especially Elizabeth, who inspired this story.
S. P.

For the Koobs ... there will always be an
extra chair for you in our home.
D. W.

First published 2015 by Walker Books Ltd
87 Vauxhall Walk, London SE11 5HJ

2 4 6 8 10 9 7 5 3 1

Text © 2009 Shirley Parenteau
Illustrations © 2009 David Walker

This book has been typeset in Journal

Printed in China

British Library Cataloguing in Publication Data:
A catalogue record for this book is available from the British Library

ISBN 978-1-4063-6453-8

www.walker.co.uk